In His Own Words

By Kenneth L. Powers, Jr.

San Marcos California 2018

Epigraph

I (Kenneth L. Powers, Jr.) began writing short stories, poems and plays in middle school. As a teen, I used writing as a vehicle to express myself. In high school, my mother encouraged me to take a newspaper writing course which led to a position as a sports writer for the high school newspaper, The Southfield Jay. As a result of hard work and dedication, I became the editor of the paper during my senior year and I received a journalism scholarship to Oakland University the following year. This book is one of my greatest achievements as a writer because it reflects my life story. As a teacher and a foster parent I believe that the issue of bullying needs to be addressed. As you read this book think about your childhood experiences with bullying and people you know who have been affected by it. This novel will also bring hope to those who are currently dealing with childhood bullying and give strategies to help them overcome it. Those who suffer from being bullied need to know that they are not alone in their struggle.

In His Own Words

Written by: Kenneth L. Powers Jr.

Published by: DFG Creative Expressions, L.L.C., San Marcos, California 2018

Dedication and Acknowledgements'

This book is dedicated to my Lord and Savior Jesus Christ; who gave me the inspiration, courage and tenacity to complete this book throughout this journey.

Next, I am also dedicating this book to my beautiful wife, Lesley M. Powers; who has encouraged me to reach for excellence and ignore my fears.

Furthermore, I am dedicating this book to my parents, Kenneth Sr. and Veronica Powers; whose guidance throughout my life has shaped me to always strive for the best in everything that I do.

Lastly, I am dedicating this book to all of the foster children who I have helped raise over the past 6 years. I hope that you will see your experiences in this book, and understand that God has a plan for your life despite the hardships that many of you have faced early in your lives.

Other positive influences who deserve an honorable mention for this book include: Bishop W.M. Thornton, Prophetess Loretta Douglas, Apostle Lee Douglas, Pastor Terrell "Rockiano" Lipsey, Eddie B. Allen, and Sherla Evans.

The Author at a glance

Kenneth Powers has 28 years of professional writing experience. As a freelance writer he has contributed to high profile Detroit based publications such as The Metro Times, The Michigan Chronicle, The Michigan Citizen, The Canton Eagle and The Hub.

He began his career writing for his high school newspaper, The Southfield Jay, at 16 years old. Later, he served as editor in chief of the high school publication which led to him receiving a partial scholarship to Oakland University. Powers also gained valuable writing experience for his college newspaper by working as a staff writer and an assistant features editor.

After college Kenneth began to pursue a career in education and has worked in the field of education for many years. "In His Own Words" is Powers' first novel. He uses his experiences working with teens and preteens for his inspiration for the book's theme of bullying.

Warning—Disclaimer

This *fictional work was created to highlight the growing problem in this country as it pertains to bullying. Moreover, this book was written to raise a heightened sensitivity to issues pertaining to bullying, and it's devastating effects on the lives of those who suffer at the hands of bullies. Written from non-actual life events of the author this book reveals the real life struggles of those who suffer in silence in a plethora of ways. Furthermore, this work was written to force a very and necessary conversation on this growing epidemic we now face. Finally, this work was created to also highlight the growing issues of the unforgotten and systemized adolescence in our society. It is sold with the understanding that the publisher and author are not engaged in rendering legal, accounting or other professional services. If legal or other expert assistance is required, the services of a competent professional should be sought.*

The purpose of this work is to educate and enlighten. The author and Para Publishing shall have neither liability nor responsibility to any person or entity with respect to any loss, or damage caused, or alleged to have been caused, directly or indirectly, by the information contained in this book.

If you do not wish to support the ideas, opinions, or *information provided in this work you may return this book in great condition to the publisher for a full refund.*

Forward

"In His Own Words" is a *fictional work that highlights life as an adopted child who has a speech impediment. The author in a very subtle way exposes the hidden issues of one particular child's life as he also reveals snapshots of his own life experiences. This work will captivate the reader, take the reader through a plethora of emotion, while forcing us as a society to deal with a very real problem with bullying. Furthermore, this work examines the struggles and hardships of those who unfortunately fall victim to the foster care system and bullying across this country. Moreover, it scrutinizes aspects of life that aren't normally portrayed in other media outlets. This work also demonstrates what happens when there is a support system willing to be the village our youth of today need. Finally, it introduces a blueprint of the inner city that displays examples of positivity through both the African American family and the church can look like. "Kudos" to author Kenneth L. Powers Jr. He should be proud of his ability to make this story come to life while strategically highlighting two very real problems in our society today."*

-Author Denaryle Lovell Williams

In His Own Words

Chapter 1

Lunchtime has always been the worst part of the day for me. I have never liked the food. It seems like we have the same thing every day: pizza, chicken, hot dogs. None of the food tastes like something we would eat at home or at a fast food restaurant. I told Mom that I wanted her to fix my lunch, but she always tells me to eat the food at school.

Another thing I hate about this time is the noise of the other kids. It is so loud sometimes I can't hear myself think. Usually I sit in the back by myself, but someone always finds their way to my table. And they always have something smart to say about my clothes or how I talk. I don't know why, but this always makes me upset. My adopted sister told me that she sees my skin turn from light brown to red whenever I get mad.

Other than getting upset easily, I think I live a regular life for a thirteen-year-old boy. I live with my adoptive parents in Detroit near the suburb of Southfield. They go to church regularly and they are always telling me that I need to control my temper, but some of these kids at my school are making it hard.

Speaking of jerks, Antuan, captain of the eighth grade basketball team and wannabe class clown, decided to join me along with a couple of his basketball flunkies, while I peacefully tried to eat my apple before this dreadful lunch period ended.

"What you got on today, Stevie?" Antuan jeered, while his three followers snickered. I didn't say anything because anybody could look at my clothes and see for themselves. But my heart started beating faster because I hate when people call me "Stevie." I prefer Steve or Steven. Only my family can call me "Stevie." After he saw that he couldn't get a response from me he continued with his games.

"I thought everybody knew baggy jeans went out of style ten or twenty years ago!" he said. "And when are you going to get some new Jordan's? Those Shaq's look like bisquits." He added, with a loud laugh, "My dad's got more swag than you!"

I couldn't take it anymore. I had to say something, even though I was so upset it was hard to get the words out. "M-m-man." I stuttered, "G-g-g-get ou-ou-ou-out of h-h-h-here."

After I said this it seemed like the entire cafeteria was laughing at me. The more I looked at Antuan and his weak goons laughing, the more upset I got. So I got out of my seat, walked up to him and punched him square in his face near his left eye, knocking him out on the cafeteria floor. One of his flunkies tried to grab me from behind, but I elbowed him in the nose, causing it to bleed. So he backed away and told the other follower to get a teacher, to stop me from hurting Antuan even more. While they went to find someone, I started stomping Antuan on his back. I felt I was giving him what he deserved: "I bet he doesn't mess with me again about my clothes or how I talk after this," I thought to myself.

"Steven Owens!" the principal called, bringing two security guards. "Stop kicking him right now!" But I *couldn't* stop. I was just getting started. I didn't want Antuan to get up. So both security guards wrestled me to the floor and handcuffed my hands behind my back. I didn't realize that it took two grown men to restrain me. I am only 5'4" and 150 pounds, but I have been working out, doing push-ups and practicing the karate moves I learned from an after-school class. I try to always be prepared before getting into a fight.

Here we go again. It seems like I am always heading to the principal's office. Whenever the secretary sees me come into the office she sits back and shakes her head. It seems like she always knows what happened before anyone tells her. "So we have to call your Mom because you are fighting again?" Ms. Johnson asks with that same look on her face. "How are you going to make it to high school when you are always getting suspended?"

Today I wasn't worried about high school, the fight or anything else. I was worried about what my adoptive mother would do when she found out I messed up again and couldn't control my temper. And on today of all days! Today she was graduating from college! It is a huge deal around our house. My adopted brother is coming home from school and everybody is getting dressed up. My adoptive dad even took off work.

"Ms. Johnson, you won't be able to reach Mom today," I explained. "She is out of town on work business."

"We will see about that," Ms. Johnson quickly answered.

I guess today was my lucky day, because my mother – who I have been living with since I came to her through foster care at three years old –

didn't answer the phone. After Ms. Johnson couldn't reach her she left Mom a message about my being suspended and saying she had to come to the school before I could return to class. I had to wait in the small, cramped office and sit on the hard, black chair in the office lobby for two hours after school. Antuan's mom had come to the school to pick him up right after lunch and I was left there with nothing but time to think. I thought about how disappointed Mom and Dad would be when they found out. I thought about the punishment I received the last time I got into a fight. I couldn't go outside for a whole week and they took my phone for two weeks. I dreaded what the punishment would be this time.

To avoid getting into another fight with some of Antuan's friends, I decided to walk home instead of taking the bus. I got to the house late and everybody was all dressed, waiting for me.

"Boy, where have you been? You should have gotten here a half-hour ago."

"Mom, I walked today." I told her, looking at the floor.

"Well we will get to the bottom of this later. You see your brother and sister are already dressed. We've gotta go. Hurry up!"

I knew Mom did not want anything to get in the way of her big day. She studied hard at the online school for four years and now she'd finally gotten her degree in social work. On the way to the stairs I ran into my sarcastic, older brother, who thinks he is so cool since he made the basketball team at University of Michigan.

"So what happened this time, you little scrub?" he laughed.

"Nothing," I said as I pushed past him to get to my room, so I could change into my dress clothes.

"I know something is up. It's just a matter of time before I find out," he said with a smirk.

"Stay the hell out of my business!" I yelled.

"Do I hear cursing in my house?" Dad asked as he came up the stairs. He was fully dressed in a gray, pinstriped suit with a matching bow tie and polished black dress shoes.

"No, sir," I told Dad. I knew Dad never used curse words, even when he got mad at me, Paul Jr. or Angel. Since Dad became a minister, he constantly tells us how to act like Christians, even though we do our own thing when he isn't around.

"Paul, get out of here," Dad said, looking into the bedroom. "It's time to go. And Steve, you have five minutes to get dressed, brush your teeth and get in the car." As I rushed to get ready to join everyone, I was kind of relieved that Mom was so busy she didn't get the call from the office on this special day. I didn't want to ruin our family's celebration just because I couldn't control my temper again.

Chapter 2

We got home late that night, around ten o'clock. Even though Mom was tired of walking around in that black cap and gown, I had never seen her so happy. She had that same smile on her face at my adoption party when I turned five years old. I remember it like it was yesterday. Everyone at my house came to this nice restaurant and sat at a long table. I think it was a private party, because my family were the only people there. The room was filled with my new grandparents, cousins, uncles and aunties, even godparents. Everybody greeted me with a hug or a gift. I still have some toys left from that day, even though I couldn't fit them all in one room back then.

Angel, my little sister, was already asleep and Paul had just left. He told Mom and Dad he was meeting some girl and he would be back before twelve. I guess when you get in college you have fun and live kind of like you are an adult. The night seemed to be winding down peacefully, but I could imagine the smile disappearing from Mom's face as she played her cell phone message and I overheard her and Dad talking, while I was in my room.

"Paul, come here and listen to this," she said. "The boy has got himself suspended again. I can't believe it. And he went on today like nothing happened. He's not going to see that cell phone until next semester. Just wait until I…"

"No need worrying yourself with this tonight," Dad said. "It's late and time for us to get some rest."

The next morning, I found my way from home to that place I hated – the principal's office. It felt funny coming to the school in the middle of the day. As I walked to the principal's office with Mom everybody kept staring at me like I was some kind of freak. I stared back and I think most of them got the message. As we went into Mr. Tolliver's office for the hundredth time, I got myself all ready for the typical scene: My Mom was going to tell Mr. Tolliver how she apologized for my behavior and how it would never happen again. She was also going to strong-arm me into an apology for beating the crap out of Antuan and make me promise to control myself. Then Mr. Tolliver would look at me for a long time and tell me I could come back in a day or two. That's how it usually happened, but I was in for a surprise this time.

When we walked into the office I saw this new lady sitting across from Mr. Tolliver's desk. She seemed to be a little younger than Mom and Mr. Tolliver. She had a pretty face and she seemed upbeat.

"Mrs. Owens and Steve, how are you today?" Mr. Tolliver asked. "I asked our new social worker, Ms. Alexander to join us. Ms. Alexander, meet Mrs. Owens and her son Steven Owens." She shook our hands firmly and smiled while greeting us.

I wasn't used to this, because most school staff just looked at us with a frown or a blank expression, so you never knew what they thought about you. Before I could sit down I was already wondering what this was all going to be about. Why was this cute, yet serious-looking, lady here?

"I am glad you came, Mrs. Owens," Mr. Tolliver said, "and we will not keep you here for a long time." Mr. Tolliver could be cool sometimes, like the night he came to the school sleepover and played video games with us. He stayed there the whole time. I like principals who show that adults can have fun, too. He didn't really seem to be in a fun mood now, because he told Mom, "We are concerned about your son's behavior. He has been suspended from school for fighting four times this month. And let's not count the other twelve times he has fought this year. Usually the other child ends up being hurt."

"Mr. Tolliver, my husband and I do not condone violent behavior in our home and we have talked to Steve about this, but my son says he is constantly being bullied because of his speech problem. What is the school doing about that?" Mom asked. Mom could be direct when she thought someone was treating us unfairly. She has even shown her feisty side in church. I remember a time when the pastor's kids were talking about Angel because she used to be cross-eyed. Mom confronted the pastor, his wife and his kids. After this happened we didn't go to church for almost a month until the pastor and his family all apologized to Angel.

"Bullying is a problem at our school and we are working on it," Mr. Tolliver said with this real serious look, as he rubbed his hand over his slick, bald head. "But we need your son to…"

"My son is tired of it all," Mom said as she started to cry. Her tears surprised me.

"Mrs. Owens, I am going to be providing services so our building can continue to be a thriving school," Ms. Alexander said. "You mentioned before that your son has a speech problem."

"Yes. He has been stuttering ever since he came to us at three years old."

"So he is in foster care?" Ms. Alexander asked.

"No, he is adopted. We adopted him when he turned five."

"So he is adopted *and* has a speech problem," Ms. Alexander said, thinking. "I need to start seeing him. A lot of students who have these types of issues get into trouble. That is why our school has need of social workers. I can put him on my schedule as soon as possible. Is that okay with you?"

"I am open to anything at this point," Mom said. "I am tired of him getting in trouble. He's got too much potential for that."

I always hated it when Mom started talking about my problems. Sometimes I talked like everybody else, other times it was just hard to get the words out. It feels like I get stuck sometimes, especially on words that have the "s" or "t" sound. I wished Mom had never brought this up. Now I'd have to see this lady every week and talk about why I couldn't get these stupid words to come out. Thanks a lot, Mom.

Chapter 3

After dealing with Mom and the new social worker I found myself looking forward to church. Dad says I'm "beyond my years" because I understand and appreciate what goes on during the service. Ever since I started playing the keyboard there, church began to make more sense to me. My Dad taught me everything I know about how to play the keyboard. He started giving me lessons right after I got adopted, and it never seemed hard for me to learn. Dad taught me how to listen to God and ask Him which keys to play during the service. So I made a practice of praying and asking God to lead me to the right keys and help me make the right sounds with my fingers. But I was shocked when Dad asked me to lead the prayer last week at our youth service.

"Praise the Lord, saints!" he called out to the congregation.

"Praise the Lord, Minister Owens!" the congregation replied.

"Today our youth are facing so much, even in the first few weeks of school. So many of them do not know the way. It's up to our children in this church to be the examples unsaved children need. And when I think about church leadership I think about my son, Steven. Steven has been such a blessing to our church over the years, playing the keyboard. But I think it's time that we hear from him. Steven, come lead the congregation in an opening prayer."

I started nervously coughing after dad asked me to leave the keyboard and come to the pulpit. He knew I had problems speaking to people sometimes, even in short conversations, especially if I felt uncomfortable. How could I lead a whole room full of youth and their parents in prayer? I locked eyes with Dad, trying to signal him to call on someone else, but he had that insistent look on his face, like he did when I tried to talk him out of making me finish my dinner or homework. After realizing Dad was serious and that all eyes were on me, I walked slowly toward the pulpit, trying to think about what I was going to say. When I finally reached the microphone I stood silently as my whole body started shaking before I could get the first word out. So I said a silent prayer to myself, asking God to help me so I wouldn't start stuttering and embarrass myself in front of everyone. It seemed like God answered my prayer and a cool breeze came over my forehead to soothe the heat and dry all the sweat that drenched my shaking body.

Finally, I felt the courage to say: "Praise the Lord, saints! Let's bow our heads and pray. Heavenly Father, we pray for all of the youth across the land, that they would know you as the forgiver of their sins and their deliverer at a young age. God, help us make the right decisions and help us honor you in our everyday lives. We thank you for our pastor and for our youth minister. Bless our service and allow us to be a blessing to someone today. In Jesus' name, Amen!"

After sitting down I don't remember the rest of the service. The only thing I remember is that Joseph, one of our teen youth ministers, got up to speak. I was feeling relieved that I got through the prayer without stuttering or messing up my words. If I could only speak that well while talking to people every day...

When it was time to leave church that day I started shutting down the keyboard to pack up and Dad came next to me, giving me this tight hug. "I knew you could do it, son," he said with this big, weird grin on his face.

"I guess so," I added, feeling confused.

"You see, if you put your trust in the Lord, all things are possible, just like the scripture says," Dad told me. "Your mother and me are looking for you to do well in school this year, and stop this fighting."

"But Dad, they are the ones always starting it!" I exclaimed.

"You have to learn how to fight back with words, not your fists. It's like a game they're playing with you. They get you worked up, talk about your speech and you get mad and beat them up. Son, I'm just saying you have to learn how to express yourself." He patted me on the head and let me finish packing my instrument.

I didn't say much because I know Dad means well. He thinks God solves all of our problems, but I knew how to make some of the jerks in school leave me alone. They would learn their lesson if they kept picking on me. Even after facing a new challenge that day at church, I felt most comfortable handling my old challenges the usual way. I've been fighting with my fists for most of my life and that's how I planned to keep dealing with bullies.

Chapter 4

When I first woke up, I knew something bad was going to happen. I felt just like my Mom, who always has a way to tell when me or my brother, or sister, are lying. Some people call it a sixth sense, but my Dad calls it hearing from God. I still seemed to be having a good day until I went to the bathroom during fourth period. I was able to get out of class, even though old, mean Ms. Brown doesn't usually let people go until the bell rings. Anyway, I think it's true what people say about being at the wrong place at the wrong time. After using the restroom and heading for the door, I noticed Antuan and three of his stupid friends coming to block me from leaving.

"What's up, tough guy?" asked DeAndre, one of Antuan's lanky, close to six-feet-tall friends.

"Hey, I don't have time for this. Ms. Brown wants me to get back to class," I said, looking at him with a hard stare.

"Who you looking at, freak?" Romeo, his stumpy friend, demanded.

"I-I-I'm looking at a f-f-f-fool!" I said, suddenly stuttering. For the next few minutes all three of the idiots just laughed.

As I clenched my fist, the only feeling that I could recognize was anger. Even though there were three boys who were clearly bigger than me and ready to pounce on me like a cat on a mouse, I was ready for them.

Before I could take my first swing, someone came in and knocked Antuan to the ground with a loud thump on his head. Someone else had Romeo in a headlock and slammed him. Romeo did not waste time leaving the restroom after seeing that his plan to beat me down was thwarted. This left me with Ellis, a skinny guy who was my size. After I pushed Ellis into the wall, he decided to leave the restroom, too. The only one there now was DeAndre and he was lying on the floor with his eyes closed – not moving.

"Get up and get outta here!" one of my helpers said as he kicked the boy in his side. When DeAndre started coughing, I was relieved. I was thinking he was really hurt. When he finally stood up, my helper gave him a shove. "And you better not tell anybody what happened here. You hear me?" added the first helper, a boy my age who was a little taller than me. Well, DeAndre didn't say anything. He just darted out of the restroom like he'd seen a ghost.

"What's up, man?" the helper nodded to me.

"Hey, thanks. I thought I had to handle those fools all by myself," I told him. The helper looked at his friend and let out a laugh.

"All by yourself? Man, you got heart. What's your name?"

"I'm Steve. How about you?"

"Deante, but call me 'D,'" he said. Later, after asking around, I found out D was new to our school. I also learned that he was in foster care like I'd been before the Owens family adopted me. This helped me feel at ease around him.

"Well, dude. I'll see you later," D said as he swaggered out of the restroom with his friend.

After going back to class, I couldn't help but think about how D helped me with those guys. For as long as I could remember, I had always fought my battles by myself. I guess that's how I got so good at fighting. I haven't lost a fight since the second grade. But I liked the idea of having help when it came to facing people who were always picking on me.

I ran into D again in the cafeteria at lunchtime. He was surrounded by pretty girls and some of the worst-behaved kids in the school, sitting at the same table.

"Hey, Steve. Come over here," Deante called to me. I agreed and walked over to their table. This was a change for me, because I usually eat by myself. "Everybody, this is Steve," D said. "Me and him had to handle some fools who tried to pop off in the restroom. He knows how to handle his business."

My hands were sweaty and I was shaking from nervousness. I don't remember, but I must have stuttered when meeting D's group.

"Why do he talk so funny?" CJ, one of D's friends asked him.

"He just gets nervous sometimes, but I can tell he's cool," D said. It felt good to hear someone defend me rather than make fun of my speech. I was also happy to see one of the girls named Lisa taking an interest in me at the table.

When the five-minute bell rang I finally got a chance to talk to D again. "Man, you can always eat at our table," he said. "You don't have to sit by yourself."

"Okay, thanks. What class are you going to next hour?" I asked him.

"I've got algebra, but I'm not going to it. Me and my boys got business at the high school. Maybe one day you can check it out," he said.

"Well…" I hesitated.

"I know you are one of those good guys, so I'll see you later. And, by the way, you need to talk to Lisa. I think she likes you."

"Okay. See you later, man," I told him. D and three of his friends walked out of the back door of the school.

Chapter 5

My report card was what I expected: My grades were not good at all. Mom was talking about me getting into Cass Technical High School, the school for the smart kids, but I didn't think I would make it. I got a D in math and I failed science and English again. I did pretty good in my electives, since I got B's in computers and gym class. And I guessed Dad would be proud of me for getting an A in music, but I didn't think I would be able to stay on the school band with the grades I got this semester.

"Steven, where is your report card?" Mom called up to my room.

"Coming," I said. As I gave her the report card I felt the same nervousness as when I had to give a speech or talk to a cute girl.

"Two F's! I can't believe this! Steven, you know that this is not acceptable.

"Yeah, Mom. But..."

"Your English teacher said you were making some improvements and the science teacher didn't say anything about failing," she added as she sat down. She looked intensely at the report card.

"I know, but English sometimes seems so hard to me."

"Steven, your problem is that you are always in the middle of something. You're always fighting and worried about those kids who are teasing you."

"Mom, I know how to handle them," I told her.

"But you can't go through life beating everybody up. You've got to find other ways to fight. With this type of report card, you know that you're grounded. You are going to spend a lot more time studying than messing around with that saxophone and playing the keyboard at church," she told me.

After Mom said this it felt like someone had punched me in the stomach unexpectedly. "B-b-b-but, Mom…" I tried to get her to hear my side before she pronounced judgment.

"I don't understand. How come you can't be like your brother and your sister?" she snapped.

"Because n-n-n-nobody is this family understands me. P-p-p-probably because they are not my real brother and sister!" I left the room before Mom could really get to me. I think she handled my comment well because I didn't hear her hollering and screaming. While I sat in my room I thought about my real biological family. Maybe my actual mother had a temper or didn't do well in school like me. Maybe somebody in the family had this stupid speech problem that I have. I guessed I'd never know because my real mother told me to move on and be a part of the Owens family right after my fifth birthday. She was going to be in jail for a long time, so I started praying for her every night.

"Nita, this punishment is too harsh," I heard Dad tell Mom.

"So what do you propose that we do? This boy is on his way to being a delinquent. You know how young, black boys, who can't perform in school and who constantly fight, end up. There is a prison cell waiting for him if he doesn't straighten out his act," Mom said.

"But the music is something he is good at. You can't take that from him."

"I know you think music is the answer to everything, because you played, but that is not true," said Mom. "He needs to be able to perform well, academically. Look at me: I didn't finish college until I was in my forties because of the mistakes I made in my youth. I don't want that for Stevie."

"Okay. I agree with part of the punishment," Dad added. "But keep him in church and let him play the keyboard in youth ministry. Maybe he can go the semester without playing saxophone in the band."

"Alright. We will try it your way. But after school that boy will be with me in the library," Mom answered. Restlessly, I fell off to sleep.

Chapter 6

In math class I couldn't concentrate, no matter how hard I tried. I thought about being on punishment and I thought about my life. I thought about how things would be different if I didn't stutter. Would I have more friends? Would Mom love me more? I thought life would be easier if I could just get my words out. I know that everyone has some kind of problem, but I wondered, "Why me?" I'm thankful for how the Owens family opened their home to me, but I really missed my real mother. Maybe she could help me in a way Mom and Dad hadn't been able to. I guess I'd never know because she wouldn't be out of jail for ten more years. And this wasn't the first time she was caught for selling drugs. She'd been caught a few years before she had me. I guess that's the reason why she had to serve so long behind bars this time.

Since I started hanging out with Deante and his crew, the kids in school seemed to respect me a little more. After knocking out a couple of knuckleheads, I saw that some were scared of me. Others didn't like Deante, but they seemed to look up to him in a weird sort of way. Most of these kids are from the suburbs and they know Deante is real "'hood," so they don't tease him or give him any problems. Along with Lisa, three other guys, "Juice," Rudy and Joe, hang with Deante. I don't know how Lisa became part of the group, but Juice, Rudy and Joe are known to be good fighters. When Deante saw my skills in the bathroom he enlisted me as part of his clique. I guess he likes to surround himself with people who fight well.

"What's up, D?" I said to Deante after math class, noticing that he looked worried.

"Man. I don't know what I'm going to do," he told me.

"What do you mean?"

"It's my foster mom," he said.

"You're in foster care?" I asked, not wanting him to know I'd heard this already. "I was in foster care, too."

"Yeah. I've been in different homes since I was seven. My mom is on drugs. Don't know where she is, and my dad was never around. They can't even find him."

"I know how it is. Until I got with the Owens nobody wanted me. The other foster parents said I was stupid, because of my speech, and bad 'cause I got into a lot of trouble," I said.

"No offense, but I don't have this perfect family ready to adopt me. I gotta take care of me, because nobody else will. I'm getting moved out of my foster mom's house. I got thirty days."

I could tell D was really upset because he clinches his fists when he's mad. He told me he was going to the bathroom. As the eighth grade class waited in the hallway for lunch I saw Lisa walking toward me. She looked cute today, wearing her blue jean outfit. I also liked her new braided hairstyle.

"Did you hear about D?" I asked her.

"Yeah, he tells me everything," she said. "He's my cousin."

"You guys are related?" I was surprised.

"No, but his foster mom is my aunt and we are like relatives," she said.

"So why is your aunt getting rid of him?" I asked her.

"He acts like he doesn't want to be there. She's tired of him skipping class, hanging out with hoodlums and being disrespectful. Last week he stayed out all night and told her it was none of her business."

"You gotta follow the rules of the foster parents you live with," I told her.

A few minutes later D came from behind me, as if he had overheard what we were talking about.

"W-w-w-what's up?" I asked him, like I'd asked earlier. I had a feeling D was going to ask me to skip class and come to the high school with him.

"Man, calm down. I can tell you're nervous because you're stuttering," he told me. "Well I'm going to the high school and I need some back-up. I got to deliver some packages to a couple of my boys."

Lisa and I looked at each other. We both wondered what those "packages" were. I hoped D wasn't getting involved in something illegal. It felt strange when he asked me to go with him and his boys, because something inside me knew this wasn't right. I thought about the scripture

Dad liked that says "avoid the appearance of evil." But I knew I could help

D if anything happened, so I went with him to the high school.

Chapter 7

I liked looking at Ms. Alexander, but I couldn't wait until this therapy session was over. Every therapy session that I have been in seems similar, in a creepy type of way. Most of the social workers and therapists ask me the same questions: Have you ever thought of hurting yourself? Do you talk to your parents about your problems? Do you talk to your friends about how you feel? The foster parents I lived with before I went to the Owens' house had me in therapy, too. Most of the therapists were nice. I played cool games at their offices, but now I saw how it was a waste of time. Most of my friends were playing sports while I was stuck in a dumb office, talking to a therapist on "how to improve my behavior."

"Steven, your teachers say you have missed a couple of classes for the past two weeks," Ms. Alexander asked. "Where have you been?"

I knew she was going to ask me about this, so I was ready for her.

"I've been having headaches, so I've been going home early. You can ask my mom," I told her.

I knew I wouldn't get in trouble because I've been telling mom about headaches, and I told her I was coming home early while she was at work that day I went with Deante to the high school.

"Okay. Let's get back to the reason why you are here today. Let's talk about your speech. You have made a lot of improvements in class for the past few months. Have you used some of the strategies that we talked about when people tease you about stuttering?"

Those "strategies" were a bunch of bull: All Ms. Alexander told me to do was clench my fist and walk away when kids picked on me. She also told me to hold my breath and count to ten – before telling the teacher!

"I've calmed down a little," I answered. "I don't let what people say get to me." I didn't feel like telling her the real reason the kids left me alone was they were scared of Deante and my new crew. I knew she wouldn't be happy about that explanation.

"It's good that you are using your strategies, but you still need speech therapy. I want to see you improve."

"B-b-b-but... I-I-I don't think I need it. I'm d-d-doing better," I told her, struggling with my words at the worst possible time.

"Steven, you have to go. Everyone needs to improve in an area. I struggled for years with math. If I avoided math forever I would not have been to make it through college," she said.

Ms. Alexander didn't want to hear what I had to say, so I just agreed with her. Plus, I knew Mom wasn't going to let me get out of speech therapy.

"Okay. I'll go," I said. After she set the appointment with a speech therapist at one of the hospitals, I was relieved to see Lisa in the hallway.

"Hey, Steve. How are things going?" she asked.

I couldn't help but notice how pretty Lisa looked. She was wearing my favorite color, light blue. I hoped we became more than just friends someday.

"Things are okay," I said. "I was just talking to Ms. Alexander. I just love seeing her once a week." I added a sarcastic tone to the last part of my answer.

"I've never been in trouble to see the social worker. So what do you guys talk about in there?"

"My anger. Also how I need to stop knocking people out when they tease me because I stutter."

"Steve, sometimes you can take things a little too seriously. You sound fine to me, even when you have a hard time with your words," she said as she smiled at me. I always loved it when she smiled. It brought out her deep dimples and made her dark brown face look like an angel.

"So have you heard from your cousin?" I asked.

"Oh, yeah, I forgot to tell you he's having a party at his friend's house. The high school friend," she added.

I remember D telling me about a friend at the high school, this guy in the eleventh grade. I also remember this friend giving D two packages in two big envelopes. D never talks about what's in those envelopes he gets from the high school.

"So how are you going to get to the party?" I asked Lisa. "I know your mom is not going to let you go."

"Yeah, I know. I'll come up with something. My cousin is in college and she owes me a favor. Maybe she can take me and we'll come up with some story for my mom."

I wish it was that easy for me to get out of the house. My brother Paul was in college, but I knew he wouldn't help me out. Besides, his college was about an hour away from our house and he hardly ever came home. The only plan I could think of was sneaking out. D would probably need my help again if things got rough with some of his enemies.

Chapter 8

It was almost ten o'clock Friday night and I expected everyone to be preparing for bed. But when I left my room I found out Dad had called a "family night." Family night was when everyone in the house sits down and watches a movie of someone's choice. Everyone gets a turn to pick the movie, so it's fun for everyone. When I was younger I always looked forward to these nights. I remember mom making popcorn and baking brownies, my favorite snack. For this latest family night, she baked an apple pie.

"Stevie, it's your turn to pick the movie," Dad said, noticing me.

"Dad, I'm not really in the mood to watch a movie. I'm tired from studying. I'm ready to go to bed." I hoped everyone would go to their rooms for the night, so I could sneak to the party while they were asleep.

"Well, since you don't want to see a movie, I guess it's my turn. I want to watch my favorite movie of all time, *Remember the Titans*," he said.

"Aww, Dad. Not the football movie again," Angel complained.

"I watched two hours of your kid movie, *Despicable Me*," he said. "Now it's your turn to put up with me and football."

I watched about a half-hour of *Remember the Titans* and then I excused myself to my room. Mom came in with a slice of pie after I sat on my bed.

"Are you okay, Stevie?" she asked.

"I'm okay. Just tired."

"I talked to Ms. Alexander today and she told me you are doing better."

"Well, I want to get off of punishment, eventually," I answered.

"I'm really proud of you," Mom said. "You've managed to control yourself and you're not in trouble in school."

I know it took a lot for Mom to come to my room and congratulate me. She doesn't praise us often for doing well. She didn't even say anything to Paul when he graduated and managed to get into the top college in Michigan. She never complimented Angel when she finally was able to write her name on a straight line last year.

"Thanks, Mom," I told her.

"Before you turn in you can have some apple pie. Just wash your plate before you go to sleep."

As I listened to the gospel music station on my iPhone, I felt guilty about my plans to sneak out. After hearing one of my favorite worship artists I thought about the scripture that Mom talks about, something about obeying your parents and your days being long. Mothers sure know how to use the Bible to keep us kids in line! I usually try to follow what the Bible says we should do, but I really sensed D might need me tonight. I didn't want to risk losing my new friend. What if some of the high school kids tried to jump him at the party? I knew some of the guys from our crew would probably be there, but D depended on me to help in these types of situations. I had a bad feeling about it, but I knew I had to go.

I looked at my cell phone and noticed it was almost midnight. Dad usually prays before he goes to bed, but I overheard him talking with Mom.

"Did it seem like Stevie was hiding something tonight?" Mom asked.

"Well, the boy has been through a lot this semester." Dad said. "You said he is making some progress with the social worker, he's not fighting as much. I think you should just let it go."

"I still need you to talk to him. Something is on his mind," Mom said. "See if he will tell you."

"Okay. I'll talk with him on the way to church tomorrow. Good night, honey."

Finally, I was ready to get out of there. I put on my new Jordan's and my best Detroit Tigers hat. This was my first party, so I felt a little nervous. On my way to the front door, I ran into Angel.

"Where are you going?" she asked me.

"W-w-w-why are y-y-y-you up?" I asked, my heart pounding.

"You know it's too late to leave the house, Stevie."

"W-w-w-what will it take to shut you up?"

"Five bucks and a bag of Doritos."

"Okay, you got it. I'll pick up a bag from the store and I'll give you some money as soon as I start getting my allowance again." She agreed and went to bed. I hoped she wouldn't tell Mom or Dad. They would truly kill me.

It didn't take long to get to D's friend's house. It was on the east side of town. I was nervous during the whole bus ride. I passed a lot of streets I have never seen before. After walking up to his house, I was surprised. It was a nice, small brick house. It looked like it was one level – no stairs. You could hear the loud trap music blaring in the house from outside.

When I walked in I immediately felt uncomfortable, as if something would go wrong at the party. Maybe it was guilt, but it might have been that sixth sense of knowing what will happen in the future. The people at church call it "a word of knowledge" or "discernment." I saw D with his arms around two of the prettiest girls I have ever seen.

"What up Steve," he called out to me. "Come over here. Meet Rhonda and Kierra." When I walked closer I smelled beer on all of their breath. I knew we were about to have a long, interesting night.

Chapter 9

While everybody seemed to be having fun, I still felt weird. I think it was because I've never been to a party before. My parents were serious Christians. They didn't drink, smoke or do anything that most people consider normal for adults. As I walked outside to get some air from the cigarette smoke I noticed a couple of boys and girls giggling and smoking. This cigarette smoke smelled different from the smoke inside. It was strong and stunk real bad. I think it was weed. Now I knew it was time to get out of there. My thoughts were racing. I began to think about getting into trouble. What if the police came? What if Mom found out that I was arrested? What if… What if… What if... Back inside the house I looked for D, but instead I ran into Lisa. She didn't look drunk or high, but she did look like she was having a good time. I guess there was a benefit to being there, after all, even though the party was too wild for me.

"I've been looking all over for you," Lisa said. "Where have you been?" I noticed she was looking even better than usual. She had on tight, red Levis and a Polo shirt.

"I was just outside getting some air. People are doing a lot of smoking around here."

"Yeah. It's a party. You know, a lot of high school kids are here. You gotta loosen up. Come on, let's dance. I hear my favorite trap song playing," Lisa said, excitedly.

As I moved into the living room to do my version of the latest dances, I noticed what seemed like a never-ending line of people coming into the house. I remember seeing a few people from our school, mostly eighth graders. I don't think most sixth or seventh graders had the nerve to sneak out of their parents' house to party in the middle of the night. After dancing with Lisa I immediately started looking for D. I knew he was having a good time with the girls, but I kept getting that bad feeling that he might be in some kind of trouble. Mom calls this feeling the Holy Ghost. After Lisa went into the other room I got a good glimpse of some of the other pretty girls at the party. Some were short, others were tall. All of them were beautiful and most of them had on nice, tight clothes. Man, I couldn't wait until I got to high school!

Everything was calm until I heard loud yelling and screaming. I went into the room where most of the people were and they were staring at this huge, dark-skinned guy with a bat in his hand. The music stopped. Some people were recording the drama with their phones. As I inched closer, I saw that the guy with the bat was arguing with D.

"Stay outta my school!" the big, fat guy yelled. "That's my area. I'm in charge of the work up there! If I catch you up there again…"

"Look, homie, this is a free country. You ain't gon' do nothing," D said.

Then, before I could get D out of the way or hit the big dude, he swung the bat and clobbered D in the head. D fell to the ground. I stepped in front of "Twin Towers," ready to grab his bat.

"Get away from my boy!" I yelled.

I looked to see if I was going to get back-up from our crew and they were in place, ready to jump on the guy and his two partners.

"This is a joke," he said. "He got this little middle school crew thinking they going to do some-"

Before he could utter his next word I grabbed the bat and we struggled with it for a while before one of his boys hit me in the back of the head with another bat. A couple of our friends were able to stop the other guys from killing all of us, by trying to rough them up. The next thing I remember is sirens and Lisa standing over me, asking if I was okay.

Chapter 10

As I sat up, I noticed the police taking people away in handcuffs. Lisa was still beside me, but her cousin was able to whisk her away before the cops started asking her questions. Lisa told me to call her as soon as I got to the hospital. Everything was fuzzy after she left, but I do remember a short, white police officer asking me questions. He asked for my parents' phone number and said he was going to call an ambulance for me. Reluctantly, I gave him my phone number. I knew my mother would kill me after finding out I snuck out and went to a wild party. I woke up later in a hospital bed. My pounding headache felt a little better. I looked around and saw my mother pacing the room. My father's head hung toward the floor and his hands were in a praying position. Shortly after I woke up, my mother gave me the tightest hug I remember getting, since I was little. After she let me go the doctor walked in.

He shined a light into my eyes and checked my pulse. He was a tall, older man with a serious demeanor: "Everything looks okay. He just has a mild concussion. Just stop by the desk before you guys leave."

The drive home from the hospital was unusually quiet. Neither of my parents showed any facial expression. They didn't ask me how I felt, even though I could still feel this huge lump in the back of my head. As the gospel music played, the only thing I could think about was D. I wondered if he was alright after being clubbed with that baseball bat. When I got up off of the floor at the party I didn't see any signs of him. I wished I had been able to stop those punks earlier.

Things continued to get weird after I got home. After taking a short nap, I found out that Mom made my favorite meal, spaghetti with extra cheese and Italian salad. Things weren't perfect because my sister made it her business to tease me about sneaking out of the house. Other than that we had a silent, peaceful meal. But the next morning I realized my homecoming was over. Even though it was a school day, no one woke me up to tell me breakfast was ready. Also, my parents didn't go to work, but they dropped Angel off at school. When I went downstairs to pour my cereal they finally greeted me and said their first words about the incident.

"Well, Steve, I heard from the police last night," Mom said. She was standing in the kitchen wearing blue jeans and a University of Michigan shirt. Usually, she wears a skirt with black flats on when she's going to work. I kept silent.

"Don't you want to know what it was about, since you're hanging out with thugs and fighting at wild parties?" she sneered. "It's time for you to learn how to deal with the police."

"Mom, I can explain."

"Explain what?" she asked, raising her voice. "How you just snuck out of the house and went to that party? And then you're fighting with drug dealers! We didn't raise you like this!"

I looked at Dad to see his reaction. I was surprised to find out he was just as upset as Mom was.

"Don't look at me! You did this!" he yelled. The roar of his voice startled me. I hadn't heard him yell this loud since Paul was caught half-naked in his room with one of his girlfriends last year.

"Let's get back to the police," Mom interrupted. "Steven, they are coming by in an hour to get to the bottom of this mess you are in. I was able to get in contact with a sergeant on the force, who can help us. Sergeant

Banks goes to my uncle's church. I talked to him already and he's not going to press charges – it helps that you got hurt in all of the mess. But, boy, this type of carrying on has to stop!"

"I know, Mom," I told her, hoping she would get off of my case. But, of course, she continued.

"I heard you were sticking up for this troublemaking foster kid at your school. I don't want you anywhere near him. You could have ended up in jail, fooling around with him!"

"So you know what happened to him after the party?" I asked.

"He was unconscious longer than you were. He just woke up this morning. His injuries were a lot worse than yours." I was relieved to hear that D was okay. "But they found drugs on him," Mom continued. "When he gets out of the hospital the police are taking him straight to jail."

I wanted to call D to check on him, but Mom took my iPhone. I went to my room to get ready for the sergeant's visit and I could hear footsteps coming up the stairs. When I opened the door I noticed Dad standing there with this concerned look on his face.

"I never knew you were hanging around these types of people. Tell me why." Dad said.

"Dad, I'm trying to get ready for the police." I didn't feel like talking about it, because I was worried about D going to jail and what I would say to Sergeant Banks.

"I mean we have tried to raise you to fear God. Hanging around thugs is not something that we ever wanted for you," Dad continued.

"Dad, he's a friend. You know I-I-I-I have a h-h-h-hard time making friends. Everybody is always messing with me because of the w-w-w-way I talk."

"How about the kids at church? They think like you and they're raised right. I thought you were friendly with them."

"B-b-b-but those kids are different. Th-th-they look at me like I-I-I'm crazy when I talk. Nobody there h-h-h-has mothers in jail. And, at least, I was able to h-h-h-help D. Fighting is something I'm g-g-g-good at."

"'Good at?' How about music? God has blessed you with musical talent."

Before I could respond to Dad the doorbell rang. It was the sergeant. I felt relieved because I didn't feel like arguing with Dad. The sergeant came in, looking neat. His uniform was pressed and crispy-clean. He was about Mom's and Dad's age, but he still had this youthful swagger about him. He seemed nice, but I knew he had a job to do. He met with me privately while Mom and Dad stayed in the kitchen. We talked for a while. He told me how he got in trouble when he was young. He said he smoked weed and ran with the wrong crowd until God saved him twenty years ago. Now he was a cop supporting his family.

He asked me questions about the night of the party and the boys who clobbered me and D. I gave him the best description of those clowns I could remember. Then he began to ask questions about D. He asked me how long I knew him and he asked about drugs. I told him I never saw D with drugs – but I didn't tell the sergeant I always had the feeling D sold them, because he always had a bankroll of cash. When the sergeant left our house I went to my room and prayed for the longest time I could remember. I prayed for D and I prayed that my parents would stop being upset with me and understand my point of view. After praying, I felt peaceful because, even with all the trouble I'd had in life, I knew God could do anything.

Chapter 11

I was relieved when I got back to school. I was tired of hearing lectures from Mom and it felt weird the way Dad kept staring at me. He looked like he was really concerned. I think the students looked at me different after the party, too. A lot of them heard about what happened to me and D. Before the party I was known as the short weirdo who stuttered and was mad at everybody all the time. Now I was the rebel who had the nerve to fight a couple of high school gangsters. It seemed like all the guys gave me a cool nod now and the girls went out of their way to smile and speak to me. As much as I liked the attention I was getting, I missed my old crew, especially D and Lisa, who I hadn't seen since that night. So I went to Lisa's locker and saw her talking to a couple of girls from her class.

"Hey, Lisa," I greeted her.

"Hey, Steve. You're looking better. I was so scared the last time I saw you. The lump on the back of your head was so big."

"I'm okay. Of course, I got grounded for sneaking out of the house. Anyway, how is D? I can't call him because my Mom took my phone."

"Things got bad for him after he got out of the hospital. He got put in jail for having weed. Luckily, he got moved into a group home, but it's still like jail – he can't leave there. He's got school in there and everything."

I could tell Lisa felt bad for him. They were close and, for me, he was like a brother. I thought about D the rest of the school day. Maybe this was a better situation for him. I knew the staff at the group home kept a close eye on him, so he wouldn't be able to sell drugs at high schools anymore.

During fifth hour I felt a little relieved because it was right after lunch and almost the end of the school day. The office called my name over the intercom, telling me to report to Ms. Alexander's office. As I put away my notebook, I began thinking about why they were calling me to meet with Ms. Alexander. We didn't have an appointment. Then I remembered this was my first day coming back to school since the party. She probably wanted to get some information out of me about D and the boys who jumped us. When I opened the door to her office I was shocked to see Mom sitting in my usual seat and Dad sitting in a chair next to her.

"Steve, come and have a seat next to your father," Ms. Alexander said with this strange smile on her face.

Before coming to the office I had a slight headache, but now my head was hurting and I had a stomach ache, too. While going to my seat there was a weird silence in the air. Everyone looked so serious.

"Don't mind us. We're just here to collect that five million dollars you won from your last fight, Mr. Mayweather, I mean Steven," Dad said with a chuckle. I guess his joke worked, because he had my uptight Mom and my counselor in stitches for a minute. One of the things I've always liked about Dad is he knows how to lighten the mood with his humor.

"Everyone, I've called this meeting to come to an agreement for a possible treatment plan for Steven, and to review the progress that we've made," Ms. Alexander said. "Let's start with some of the progress that he's made in the last four months. First of all, his grades have picked up. He is receiving passing grades in his core subjects, literature and pre-algebra." I guess all that after-school tutoring paid off. I looked at Mom as she wiped sweat from the top of her forehead. I guess she was relieved. "But, as we all know," Ms. Alexander continued, "there are still areas Steven needs to work on. First, let's talk about that party you went to two weeks ago." She was looking straight into my eyes. I tried to look away, but she didn't blink.

"What do you want to know?"

"You snuck out of the house late at night and you went to a wild party with high school students, not to mention getting severely hurt. What were you thinking?"

"Well, I knew my parents wouldn't let me go, and my friends were going to be there," I told her.

"Mrs. Owens, do you know about these friends, particularly Deante Johnson? He's an eighth-grade foster student who came to our school a few months ago."

"Yes," Mom answered. "I know about him now, after the party, but Stevie has never mentioned him. The only friends we knew about were the kids from our church."

"I find this interesting," said Ms. Alexander, "but it isn't unusual for most teenagers. Steven, you have close friends that your parents don't even know, but you risked hurting a lot of them with your violent behavior. Why do they mean so to you that you would sneak out of the house to be with them and get into all of this trouble?"

"D is one of the only friends I ever had," I explained. "He never judged me. He never made fun of my speech and I felt like I was part of something." I tried to avoid looking at Mom as I spoke.

"But you do belong to something: You're part of our family," she said with this tear in her eye.

"And how about the church?" Dad asked. "You belong to the church and there's plenty of young people there who are on the right track."

"Dad, we've talked about this before. The kids at church just don't get me," I said, raising my voice.

"Alright," Ms. Alexander said. "We're not here for a fight. Obviously, Steven has strong feelings about his friends and you obviously don't want him hanging around people who are always getting into trouble. I think part of the problem, Steven, is that you need to learn how to make friends. I mean *positive* friends, people who are doing some of the same things you like to do. Now that your grades have improved, maybe you can get back involved in the band. The band instructor told me you're one of their best saxophone players."

"Maybe you're right, but I don't know where to start," I said. "People think I'm..."

"Stop right there, Steven," she told me. "Part of your problem is that you worry too much about what people think. Everybody doesn't think bad of you or tease you because of the way you talk. Some people see past that."

I never thought people saw past the way I spoke until I met D and Lisa. I wondered if I could really find friends who were doing the right things and who wouldn't focus on my speech problem. Before the meeting ended I apologized for being rude to my parents. Ms. Alexander talked to us about a therapist who specializes in anger management and who might help me. I felt pretty good after this appointment. It was the first time I felt like this therapy stuff helped me.

Chapter 12

It's been a couple of months since that last meeting with Ms. Alexander and it seems like my life has changed. I've been thinking about what she said about making friends and not worrying about what everybody thinks of me. A few weeks after that, my mother started taking me to a speech therapist and it wasn't as bad as I thought it would be. The speech therapist was a cool guy and we talked about ways to help me speak clearly without stuttering. He taught me how to slow down my speech and "ease into words" when I felt like I couldn't get them out. It also helped that I got some anxiety pills from my other therapist, so I could calm down when talking to other people.

In speech therapy there are other kids who have the same problem as me. We meet once a month and talk in an environment where we can stutter without worrying about people laughing at us. I met a new friend named Fred and we seemed to hit it off. He likes drawing and his jokes always crack me up. Two weeks ago I spent the night at his house, with my parents' permission.

School has been okay. I haven't gotten into a fight since the night of the party. I've been focusing my attention on the band, so I don't have time to get into it with people. We have band practice every day and my teacher recently made me the leader of my section. I haven't talked much to D's crew since the party. I heard one of the guys, CJ, got suspended for fighting last week, so I've tried to keep my distance to stay out of trouble. The only one I see often is Lisa. As a matter of fact, Lisa and I decided to make our relationship official when I asked her to be my girlfriend. She said yes and it was one of the best days of my life. My last report card was better because I managed to pull up the old D grades to C's – and I was no longer failing language arts after I got a C-.

I wasn't able to get into Cass Technical, so Mom was disappointed, but my band teacher helped me get into a good school called Ferndale High. Dad was excited because I'll be one of the freshman band leaders, which was one of the reasons Mom went along with letting me go there. Lisa and I reached out to D and he is doing better, too. He was able to get into a football program at the group home. Besides "hustling," playing sports was something he liked and was good at. We visited D at the group home a few weeks ago. He complained about the food and he was stressed out about money, but I could tell he was doing better. I told him not to worry because he would be able to get a legal job when he turned fifteen in a few months. He was excited about being able to go to the neighborhood's "alternative" high school in Detroit. The football coach there had been trying to recruit him.

Everything was going great for me and my friends until the last day of school. Lisa and I were holding hands right before the last period of the day and Antuan came up to us with some stupid remarks.

"So, Lisa, what are you doing hanging around this weird freak? All he does is throw things and hit people, because he can't talk. Isn't that right, Stevie?" he jeered.

My stomach started hurting and I could feel the tension in my throat as I felt like giving him a piece of my mind, but I couldn't say the first word to him.

Lisa looked at me and I knew she could sense I was upset, ready to fight again.

"You know what?" she said, staring at him. "I don't know what Keshia sees in you. Even though you think you're all that because you're on the basketball team, she is your *first* girlfriend. All the other girls look at you and see how ugly you are. So don't hate on Steve because he looks better than you."

"Leave me the hell alone, Lisa!" he shouted. "Both of you are nobodies. You probably deserve each other!"

Before Lisa or I could respond he walked away, like a little punk. I guess it pays to have a cute girl who has your back.

"Steve, you see what I just did," Lisa said with a grin. "I told him off without having to throw a punch."

"Yeah," I said. "That was good."

"These jocks think they're all that just because they play basketball, but most of them are insecure. There is plenty you can say about them without hitting them," she added.

Well, I thought to myself, this was easier said than done. But next time I get into it with one of those bullies, I'm going to take her advice.

And I've been using those strategies from anger management and speech therapy, so I'm learning how to calm myself down. With God on my side, I know I can do it. I can stay out of trouble and enjoy my high school years. They're supposed to be the best of my life.

...The End

www.ingramcontent.com/pod-product-compliance
Lightning Source LLC
Chambersburg PA
CBHW060236180626
46813CB00007B/3107